The Big Yawn

Also by Sonja Bougaeva: *The Visitor* (Gecko Press 2007)

English translation © Gecko Press 2009

Translation Monika Smith
Adapted by Sophie Huber and Penelope Todd

English edition first published in Australia and New Zealand in 2009 by Gecko Press
PO Box 9335, Marion Square, Wellington 6141, New Zealand
Email: info@geckopress.com

National Library of New Zealand Cataloguing-in-Publication Data

Spang, Monika 1970-
Große Gähnen. English
The big yawn / Monika Spang ; illustrated by Sonja Bougaeva.
ISBN 978-1-87746-718-9 (hbk.) — ISBN 978-1-87746719-6 (pbk.)
[1. Zoo animals—Fiction. 2. Bedtime—Fiction. 3. Yawning—Fiction.]
I. Bougaeva, Sonja, 1975- II. Title.
833.914—dc 22

Typesetting: Vida Kelly Design
Printing: Everbest, China

Paperback 978-1-877467-19-6
Hardback 978-1-877467-18-9

For more curiously good books, please visit www.geckopress.com

GECKO PRESS

The Big Yawn

Written by Monika Spang   Illustrated by **Sonja Bougaeva**

GECKO PRESS

Quickly now, it's almost eight.
We're the last ones through the gate.
Something happens as the sun goes down –
the most outlandish show in town.

You'll only see it at the zoo;
Watch carefully, as we walk through.

Checkmate in the tiger's cage – he wins!
At eight, a different game begins.
Tiger starts with a modest cough
(this cat's not one for showing off);
ever so slightly his left ear twitches
and there's a crinkling in his whiskers.

Then even though he's barely tired …

he yawns!

From the tiger, the yawning bug leaps to the swans,
who live nearby in a placid pond.
It's now exactly eight-o-two
and dusk is falling on the zoo.

The showy swans are upper class;
see them foxtrot on the grass?
Their shapely necks are stretching out —
they're elegant without a doubt —
but even though they'd rather not ...

they yawn!

Come from the pond to the porkers' pen;
the yawning bug will bite again.
The game's not over yet, you see
— tick-tock, the clock says eight-o-three.
The dinner leftovers go down with a slurp;
one last rummage, a noisy burp,
a bedtime scratch on the fencing rail,
a piggy twirl of a corkscrew tail,
then, lacking the bashfulness of swans ...

they yawn!

Come across now to the crocodile,
who thinks of his pond as the mighty Nile.
The bug arrives on the sandy shore,
right on the dot of eight-o-four:
the tired eyes begin to squint,
and on each lumpy cheek there glints
a salty tear.
Fearsome jaws are opened wide
— pooh! what a stink comes from inside! —

So many teeth, so many tears …

they yawn!

The cheeky hyenas are almost charming,
running about, already warming
up their voices; they just can't wait,
now it's exactly seven past eight.
They get the giggles at the end of the day,
yelping and cackling in noisy play,
crooning so horribly out of tune,
one night they'll frighten off the moon!
Nevertheless ... can you guess?

They yawn!

Now follow your noses straight ahead;
the giraffes are nearly ready for bed.
At eight-o-eight, no less, no more
(with baboons gathering at the door —
it always makes the primates chuckle,
when spindly legs begin to buckle),
the spotty necks are waving around,
heads sway and dip towards the ground.

Willing or not, there they go ...

they yawn!

From the giraffes to the donkeys' stall,
where heavy eyes begin to fall.
By the clock it's eight-o-nine;
the yawning bug bites right on time.
The donkeys are a funny pair;
their scrawny tails swish the air.
With long ears twitching at the tips,
they curl their rubbery upper lips.
And next thing, what do they do?

They yawn!

The lion's den is our final stop;
look at Leon combing his mop!
Ten past eight is grooming hour;
Lenny's had a lovely shower.
These cats like to primp and preen,
till every inch is squeaky clean.
When they're trimmed from mane to claw,
they give out their almighty roar ...
but really...

they are
yawning!

By half past eight the yawn has spread
to every pond, pen, cage and shed.
The llama, the rhino, the kangaroo,
the bear, the zebra and the gnu;

Everyone's yawning at the end of day;
settling down to hit the hay.
Some snore, some snuggle, some count sheep,
all the animals are going to sleep.

And you?